**For
Matthew, Beatrice and Francis
M.W.**

First published in Great Britain in 1991 by
Simon & Schuster Young Books
Wolsey House, Wolsey Road,
Hemel Hempstead,
Herts. HP2 4SS

Text copyright © Martin Waddell 1991
Illustrations copyright © Neil Reed 1991

Typeset in 18pt Garamond Book by Goodfellow & Egan, Cambridge
Printed and bound in Belgium by Proost International Book Production

A catalogue reference for this book is available from the British Library

ISBN 0-7500-0606-4

MARTIN WADDELL • NEIL REED
COMING HOME

SIMON & SCHUSTER
YOUNG BOOKS

I live with Mum and Dad and Grandad
in America.

One day my Grandad told my Dad,
"I want to go back home again."
"This is your home, Dad," said my Dad.
Grandad said,
"No! Back home to Ireland."

"I want to go, too," I said.
Grandad said, "Can I take Patrick?"
And Mum and Dad said, "Yes!"

We got busy.
We bought things.

Mum and Dad took us to the airport.

My yellow suitcase bust on the way and
I nearly lost my new baseball mitt.

We went on the big plane.
Grandad talked about what his home was like.
I watched movies.

Ireland was pretty much like most places,
only **wetter**.

The next day Grandad got a car and we went along the road to the west. Grandad said it was Irish big. I said it was American small.
The roads got smaller and smaller.

"This is home," said Grandad. "Tullyvey!"
Grandad's old house had no roof, so we
had to stay in Seamus Connolly's house,
down the lane.

Seamus Connolly remembered Grandad as a little boy.
They talked and talked.
I played with Liam and Bridget and little Colum.

We went everywhere.

There were no fences.

Colum fell in the bog.

I got him out.

One day I cut turf with Seamus and Grandad, and Bridget helped me to put it on the bank.

We climbed on Looney's rocks.

We played ghosts at Grandad's old house.

It was getting dark.
Grandad sent us home but he stayed behind.
We hid and watched him.

I think he was remembering.

On the last day, we fetched Martin Early's sheep
from the mountain.

We had tea in Martin Early's house.
There was a lamb and Bridget fed it
with a bottle.

Then we went back over the fields to Connolly's.
It was dark when we got there, but the house wasn't.

It was full of people saying goodbye to Grandad.

The next day we had to go.
Grandad said *Slainte* to Seamus, which means
'Good health'.

We went away.
Bridget waved to us until we couldn't see her anymore.

When I got back home, I sent Bridget
a picture of our house because
she doesn't believe we have a pool.
She sent me a postcard back.

I gave Bridget's postcard to Grandad
to stop him feeling sad.

We talk a lot about Tullyvey.
Grandad is too old to go home again.

Maybe I will go for him.

PRINTED IN BELGIUM BY

proost
INTERNATIONAL BOOK PRODUCTION